W9-BLW-863

Disney

WHAT'CHA THINK?

Written by Cynthia Stierle
Based on the series created by Michael Poryes and Rich Correll & Barry O'Brien

A girl can dream.

Reader's Digest
Children's Books®

Pleasantville, New York • Montréal, Québec • Bath, United Kingdom

The Best of Both Worlds

Miley Stewart is lucky—and not just because she's got a secret life as the famous pop star Hannah Montana! (Although that is pretty cool.) What makes Miley really lucky is having a close family and two awesome best friends, Lilly and Oliver. She can trust her friends with her big secret. But she can also rely on them to help her out with everyday problems, too—things like studying, crushes, and just fitting in at school. Of course, Lilly and Oliver know they can count on Miley, too.

Now you can have the best of both worlds....

Just like Miley, you probably check in with your friends if you need some help. But wouldn't it be great to see what Miley or her friends have to say? When you want to check in with Miley, just ask a yes or no question and press a button on the "What'cha Think?" device that comes with this book. The part-time pop star will send you a

Oliver

Lilly

"text message" letting you know exactly what she thinks. (The same goes for Lilly, Oliver, and Miley's secret-celebrity self, Hannah.)

If you can't think of any questions, don't worry. This book is filled with questions and quizzes. Read through a quiz, and if you don't know the answer right away or you just want another opinion, check in with Miley and her friends. You can even take a quiz twice, comparing your answers to theirs. And remember, it's all for fun. So if you get an answer that doesn't make you smile, don't worry. Just ask your question again. After all, nobody's perfect—even Miley and her friends make mistakes.

SECRET COVERS!

You probably dream about being a music star. . . . almost everyone does! But if you were leading a double life as the latest music sensation, what kind of music would you play? Pop music that gets the crowd on its feet? Country music that gets your fans singing along? Or would you rock the house with your awesome electric guitar solo? As you take the quiz, use your "What'cha Think?" device to check in with Hannah to see if she agrees with the answer you've picked. Then you'll know how to rock out the show.

1. **When the alarm goes off in the morning you hear:**

    music with a twang.

    music with a funky beat.

    nothing unless it's loud, real loud!

2. **Your ring tone would:**

    make you want to hum along.

    make you want to dance along.

    make heads turn.

3. **If you were singing a song with a famous band of brothers, onstage you'd:**

    share the mic as you sang a slow duet.

    perform an amazing dance routine.

    jump wildly all over the stage.

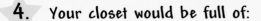
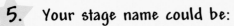

4. **Your closet would be full of:**

 pretty skirts and cute boots.

 skinny jeans and lots of bling.

⚡ graphic T's and lots of black.

5. **Your stage name could be:**

🤠 SueAnn Pecan.

👠 Ashley McFashley.

⚡ Lereign Maine.

6. **Your latest CD might be called:**

 Hearts and Home.

👠 *Hands in the Air.*

⚡ *Rock On.*

7. **You'd launch your new CD:**

 at a big ole party in Nashville.

👠 at the hottest club in LA.

⚡ at an underground club in NYC.

8. **Your tour bus would be filled with:**

🤠 all the comforts of home.

👠 all the latest tech gadgets.

⚡ lots of guitars and amps.

WHO ARE YOU?

"MOSTLY 'S:" You're a country girl at heart. You're sure to warm the hearts of all your fans with your down-home music.

"MOSTLY 'S:" You're a pop princess. The crowd is on its feet and moving to the beat of your latest hit song.

"MOSTLY ⚡ 'S:" You love rock 'n' roll! Fans everywhere play air guitar when they hear your awesome sound.

7

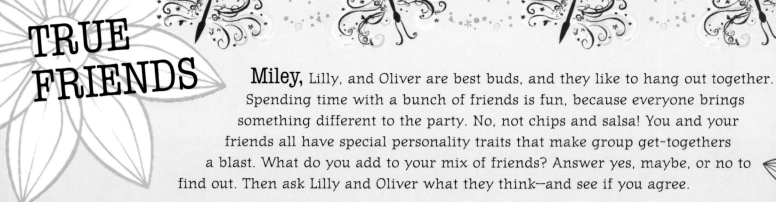

TRUE FRIENDS

Miley, Lilly, and Oliver are best buds, and they like to hang out together. Spending time with a bunch of friends is fun, because everyone brings something different to the party. No, not chips and salsa! You and your friends all have special personality traits that make group get-togethers a blast. What do you add to your mix of friends? Answer yes, maybe, or no to find out. Then ask Lilly and Oliver what they think—and see if you agree.

1. Your friend impulsively buys a wild new outfit that was in a store display. But when she tries it on, it's really . . . out there. Do you gently tell her to return it?

YES — people will probably laugh if she wears it to school.
MAYBE — but first you'll see if some changes can make it wearable.
NO — you buy one so you can both wear it on the same day. Maybe you'll start a fashion trend!

2. You've just been invited to a big party—but your best bud hasn't been asked. Do you check to see if you can bring her along?

YES — it won't be the same without her.
MAYBE — first you'll see if she wants to go.
NO — you'll just bring her anyway.

3. Your BFF just broke up with her boyfriend and you've been talking to her for an hour. She wants to keep talking, but your favorite TV show is coming on. Do you keep talking?

YES — you can catch the show some other time.
MAYBE — you offer to text her while you watch.
NO — but you encourage her to watch the show, too, to take her mind off of things.

4. OMG! Your friend walked into the cafeteria with toilet paper stuck to her shoe. She leaves right away, but texts you to make sure no one else noticed. You saw people laughing, but you're not sure what they were laughing about. You text back . . .

YES — NO1 noticed.
MAYBE — IDK
NO — a few. NBD

5. Your friend really wants to get a dog. Her 'rents have agreed if she takes care of the dog. You know your friend is a bit forgetful. When she asks you if she should get one you say:

YES — you'll text her to remind her to feed and walk it.

MAYBE — you get some dog care books to make sure she understands the responsibility.

NO — but you offer to go with her to the dog pound to walk the dogs there. Then she'll know if she's ready for her own.

6. Your friend is trying out for the cheering squad and wants you to try out, too. Backflips aren't your thing. You say:

YES — you would've had to learn how to do a backflip at some point anyway.

MAYBE — at the very least you'll cheer her on.

NO — but you'll try out for the soccer team at the same time.

7. You and your friends are deciding what movie to see. Would you pick a touching dramatic flick?

YES — those stories are always sweet.

MAYBE — if it got good reviews.

NO — you'd rather have a LOL comedy.

8. You've won concert tickets from a radio station. Two of your friends love the band, but you can only bring one. Do you flip a coin?

YES — so they'll know you don't play favorites.

MAYBE — or you'll see if they can make the decision.

NO — you'll run a silly contest for them and take the winner.

SCORING: 1 point for every YES, 2 points for every MAYBE, and 3 points for every NO.

8-13: Kind and caring. You're always aware of your friends' feelings, and you'll be there for them even if it means putting yourself out.

14-19: Loyal and level. You're a good friend, and you try to play fair all the time.

20-24: Fun and fearless. You go your own way—but your friends know it's fun to be along for the ride.

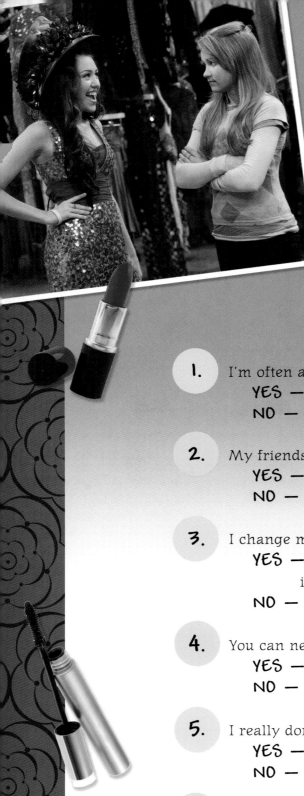

MAKE ME UP BEFORE YOU GO-GO

Miley gives herself a makeover all the time, going from an ordinary teen to pop sensation Hannah Montana. She's even given Lilly a makeover for a school dance, turning Lilly from SK8TR girl to D8TR girl. Of course, Lilly didn't really need a makeover . . . and you probably don't need one, either. But makeovers are fun, so answer yes or no to find out whether you should get one. Then get a guy's opinion; check in with Oliver to see what he thinks—and if he doesn't give you a definite answer, try again.

1. I'm often at the mall or shopping online.
  YES — I love to look at the latest styles.
  NO — my mom does my shopping.

2. My friends always want to copy my clothes.
  YES — they all like my stuff.
  NO — I have a look all my own.

3. I change my hairstyle all the time.
  YES — barrettes, hair bands, up or down, it's all fun.
  NO — it's been the same since forever.

4. You can never have too many shoes.
  YES — 'nuff said.
  NO — a pair of sneakers is all I need.

5. I really don't need much makeup.
  YES — I let me show through.
  NO — I'm under the eyeliner somewhere.

6. It doesn't take me long to do my hair in the morning.
  YES — my style is pretty simple.
  NO — I need an extra hour just for the blow-dryer.

7. I keep a nail file in my locker.
  YES — I'm ready for a nail emergency.
  NO — I usually bite them, anyway.

8. A locker mirror? A must-have.
  YES — a quick check makes me feel better.
  NO — it doesn't much matter.

9. I need to decide the night before what to wear to school.
  YES — it would take way too much time in the morning.
  NO — I could get dressed in the dark (matching is optional).

10. When I see a new style, I'll try it on even if I don't think it will work on me.
  YES — sometimes you get a nice surprise!
  NO — why bother?

SCORING: Give yourself 1 point for every YES answer.

0-3: A MINI MAKEOVER. You're comfortable with your look, but you might be overdue for a change. You don't have to change who you are, or wear things that aren't your style. But flip through a fashion magazine to see if there are some new styles that appeal to you.

4-6: MAKEOVER . . . MAYBE. You're not afraid to change some things, but you probably could use a little boost. Maybe it's time to clean out your closet to make room for a few new pieces.

7-10: MAKEOVER MAVEN. You are probably the one giving fashion advice to your friends. It's great, but if you find a style you love, don't be afraid to stick with it for a little while.

Psst! Even if you don't need to change your look, it's always fun to get together with your friends and give yourself makeovers—especially if you're having a slumber party. Buy some inexpensive hair accessories and makeup items so each guest has her own. (You already know not to share makeup and hairbrushes.) Then have fun styling the night away!

WILD WARDROBE

ADMIT IT: you'd LOVE to have a closet like Hannah Montana's! After all, she has designer clothes, juicy jewelry, and cute shoes. But if you could have any of her wardrobe—clothes, jewelry, or shoes—which would you most want to see in your closet? Follow the path to find out. Then check with Hannah Montana to see if she wants to steer you in another direction. (It is her closet, after all!)

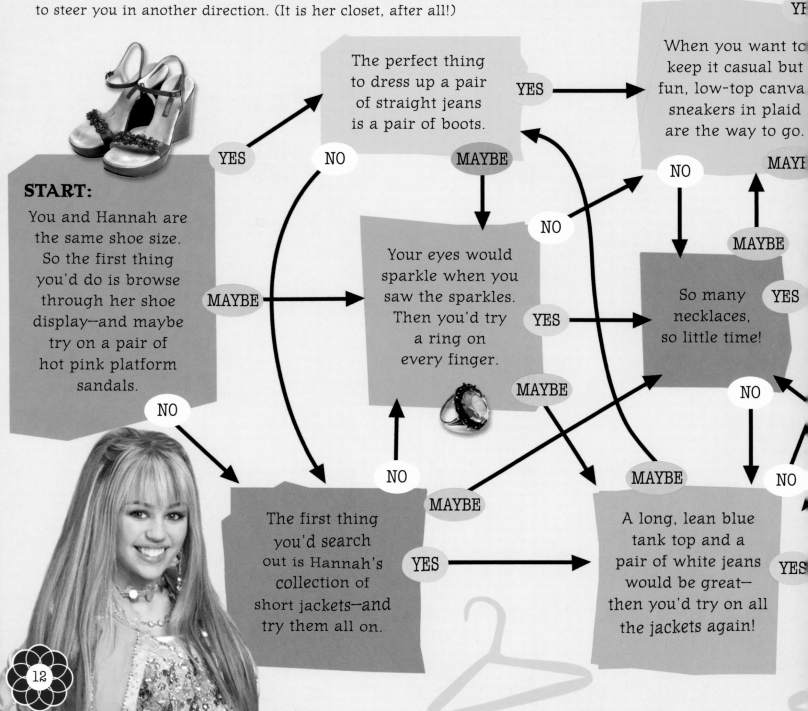

START:
You and Hannah are the same shoe size. So the first thing you'd do is browse through her shoe display—and maybe try on a pair of hot pink platform sandals.

The perfect thing to dress up a pair of straight jeans is a pair of boots.

When you want to keep it casual but fun, low-top canvas sneakers in plaid are the way to go.

Your eyes would sparkle when you saw the sparkles. Then you'd try a ring on every finger.

So many necklaces, so little time!

The first thing you'd search out is Hannah's collection of short jackets—and try them all on.

A long, lean blue tank top and a pair of white jeans would be great—then you'd try on all the jackets again!

YES   NO   MAYBE   YES   NO   MAYBE   NO   MAYBE   YES   NO   MAYBE   NO   MAYBE   YES   YES

Ballet flats in ten different colors are necessities.

YES

NO

MAYBE

NO

Hannah's metallic belts make her tanks and jeans go from everyday to blow-them-away.

YES

MAYBE

NO

MAYBE

You'd love to try on Hannah's shimmering satin dresses so you could walk the red carpet, too!

YES

THE SHOE FITS: You'd love to have Hannah's amazing collection of shoes—from colorful wedges to funky boots, your feet would have all the fun!

BLING! BLING! You'd go for the gold . . . and the silver . . . and all the sparkle in Hannah's collection of jewelry and accessories.

FASHION FEVER: Skinny jeans, flare pants, colorful tanks, hoodies, halters—Hannah's closet is better than any boutique you could imagine.

— SCHOOL ZONE —

At school Miley is just an average girl – and that's exactly what she wants to be. And like all average girls, Miley runs into everyday problems at school. You know, like the time she and Lilly found themselves at the bottom of the popularity list, right after Dandruff Danny! Since Miley knows what school is really like, you can use your "What'cha Think?" device to ask her a few questions about school, like the ones below. Then Miley will send you a "text message" so you can see what she thinks. And don't forget to check in with Lilly and Oliver, too.

1. My band concert is coming up. Will I remember what I practiced?

2. If schedules change, will I still have lunch period with some of my friends?

3. Will my locker stay organized?

4. Will I get a lot of homework?

5. Will I make lots of new friends this year?

6. Club activities are fun. Should I try a new club?

7. Is there something I'd like to eat in the cafeteria?

8. Will I be able to handle any fashion emergencies?

9. If I have to do an oral report, will I sound okay?

10. Will I ever get sent to the principal's office?

11. The school dance is coming up. Will it be a blast?

12. Should I try out for the cheerleading squad?

* Miley's Tip—

If you get an answer that makes your stomach butterflies do backflips, it's **SO** not the end of the world. The answers, like life, are what you make of them. So just ask the question again or try to put a positive spin on the answer. After all, even if you don't remember everything you've practiced for the school concert, it might mean you'll miss only one note. NBD! Or if you have to do an oral report, maybe you won't sound **OKAY**, you'll sound **FANTASTIC**!

EXERCISE, ANYONE?

Miley might not always be the best athlete in school. But maybe she's just not playing the right games. After all, exercise is great. Do you know what game is perfect for you? After you've taken the quiz for yourself, check with Oliver to find out if he agrees. Then see if you can help Miley and Lilly find their games, too.

1. You're old enough to go to the gym with your mom.
She wants to know what you'd like to do. You suggest:
 A. ditching the gym for the local skate park.
 B. taking a spinning class.
 C. running on a treadmill while she takes a yoga class.

2. When you play on a team, everyone knows that you're:
 A. in it for the fun.
 B. in it to win it.
 C. doing your best.

3. Exercising at the beach means:
 A. bodysurfing.
 B. a game of beach volleyball.
 C. going for a jog.

4. If you could win an Olympic medal, you'd want it to be in:
 A. freestyle skiing.
 B. soccer or ice hockey.
 C. individual swimming or ice-skating.

5. If you won tickets to a sporting event, you'd like to see:
 A. the X-Games.
 B. the World Cup.
 C. Wimbledon.

6. You watch sports on TV:
- **A.** when a surfing competition is on.
- **B.** whenever your fave team is playing.
- **C.** whenever your fave athlete is competing.

7. In gym class you love it when:
- **A.** you get to use the climbing wall.
- **B.** you play team games.
- **C.** you can choose your own game.

8. It feels great when:
- **A.** you create a new dance move.
- **B.** you help your team win.
- **C.** you beat your best performance.

9. The summer camp you'd like to attend is:
- **A.** an adventure camp that lets you blaze a new trail.
- **B.** a sports camp with other players from your team.
- **C.** a sailing camp that lets you sail solo.

10. If you won a gift card to a sporting-goods store, you'd buy:
- **A.** a skateboard.
- **B.** a soccer ball.
- **C.** a tennis racket.

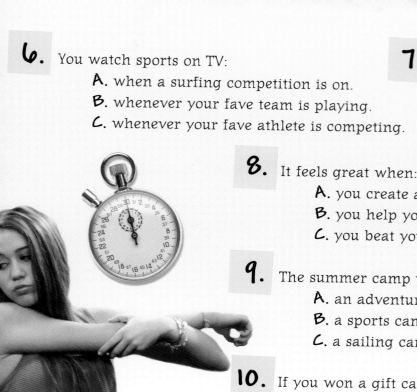

Mostly A's: X-tremely Fun. You don't move unless you're having fun—and that means everything from sports like surfing and snowboarding to dancing the night away.

Mostly B's: Go Team. You play well with others and it shows—soccer, basketball, cheerleading, or lacrosse—it's all a team effort!

Mostly C's: Flying Solo. You go solo in the spotlight, so individual sports like swimming, gymnastics, or track and field are ones that might let you shine.

17

ARE WE FAMILY?

Miley loves her dad, Robby Ray, and she thinks her brother, Jackson, is pretty great, too. (But that doesn't mean she wants to share a bathroom with him!) Of course, they both help Miley keep her identity as Hannah Montana a secret. That could make everybody crazy, but Robby Ray is pretty relaxed and keeps everything and everyone calm. What's your family like? Are they laid-back and casual? Are they always on the go? Check out this quiz and find out—then try the quiz with Miley, Lilly, and Oliver to see what they say about their families.

1. The whole family sits down for dinner every night.
   - A. YES — it's a great way to unwind.
   - B. MAYBE — more like a few times a week.
   - C. NO — unless sitting in the car counts.

2. On vacation we like to relax—at the beach, in the mountains, wherever.
   - A. YES — that's our pace.
   - B. MAYBE — but we'd also go sailing or hiking, too.
   - C. NO — you'd find us at a theme park instead.

3. In the morning our house resembles an herbal tea commercial.
   - A. YES — things are peaceful and quiet.
   - B. MAYBE — if it's a weekend.
   - C. NO — unless the commercial was shot in Grand Central Station.

4. We're always up for doing things in the spur of the moment.
   - A. YES — surprises are fun.
   - B. MAYBE — we'd have to check the schedule.
   - C. NO — the schedule is so full we don't even have to check.

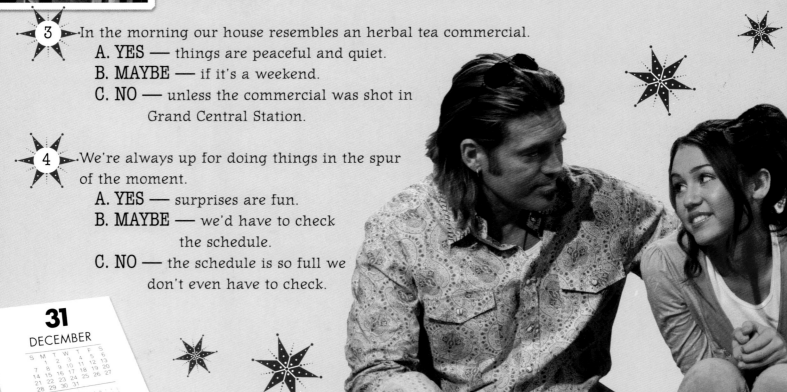

31
DECEMBER

5 My friends come to my house to chil-lax.
  A. **YES** — our house is a great hangout.
  B. **MAYBE** — I have to check with my 'rents first.
  C. **NO** — I'm usually at other people's houses.

6 A family Friday night would mean eating popcorn and playing board games.
  A. **YES** — it's a great recipe for fun.
  B. **MAYBE** — or we might go out for pizza.
  C. **NO** — we'd probably get tickets to see something instead.

7 Your family rents some DVDs. They're most likely to be for-the-whole-family comedies.
  A. **YES** — then everyone can enjoy them.
  B. **MAYBE** — sometimes we get a mix.
  C. **NO** — we each pick our own flicks.

8 The inside of the family car is neat and organized.
  A. **YES** — we're all responsible for getting our things in and out.
  B. **MAYBE** — it can get a bit messy with everyone's stuff.
  C. **NO** — we actually call our car the rolling dining room.

MOSTLY A'S:
Laid-back and Casual.
Your family is pretty relaxed about everything. While you may all be doing different things, you definitely set aside some time for everyone to be together and relax. But don't forget that playing together can be as much fun as relaxing together.

MOSTLY B'S:
Middle of the Road.
You've all got places to go, but that doesn't mean you don't want to take a time-out once in a while to hang with the people you love.

MOSTLY C'S:
Always on the Go.
Your family is involved in lots of different things, so you're all pulled in different directions. All the activity is great, but don't forget to take some time to just chill together.

COUNTRY ROADS...WHERE'S MY HOME?

Miley and her family moved from Tennessee to Malibu, California. They went from a view of the mountains to a view of the Pacific Ocean. Have you ever wondered if the view out of your front window would change? Where would you like live: in the country, in the city, or at the beach? Follow the path as you answer each question, or check with Lilly or Oliver to see if they know where you should relocate to someday.

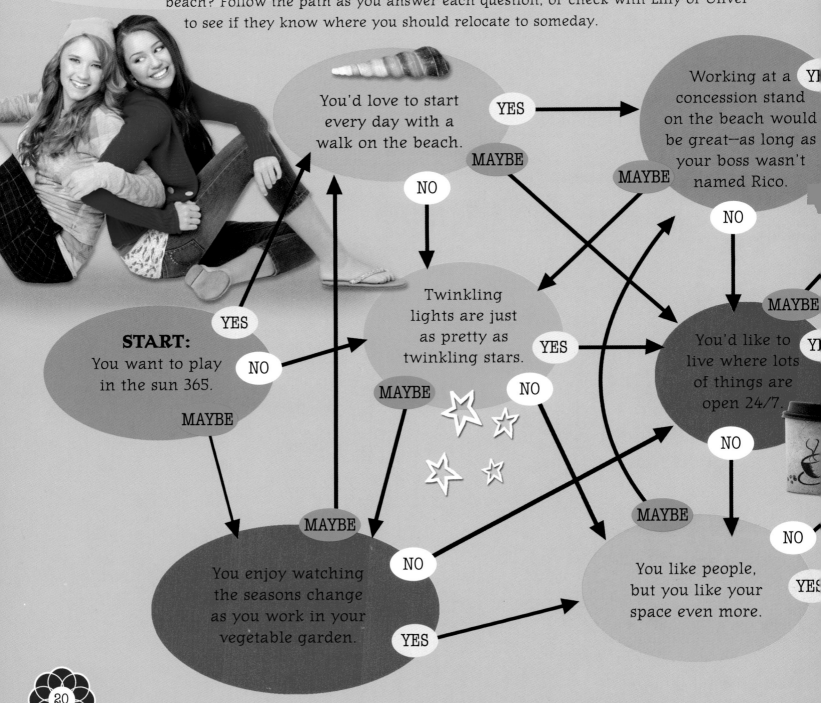

You'd love to start every day with a walk on the beach.

YES

Working at a concession stand on the beach would be great—as long as your boss wasn't named Rico.

MAYBE

MAYBE

NO

NO

START:
You want to play in the sun 365.

YES

NO

Twinkling lights are just as pretty as twinkling stars.

YES

You'd like to live where lots of things are open 24/7.

MAYBE

MAYBE

NO

MAYBE

NO

MAYBE

You enjoy watching the seasons change as you work in your vegetable garden.

NO

NO

YES

You like people, but you like your space even more.

YES

The only car you've ever really wanted is a convertible.

YES

MAYBE

NO

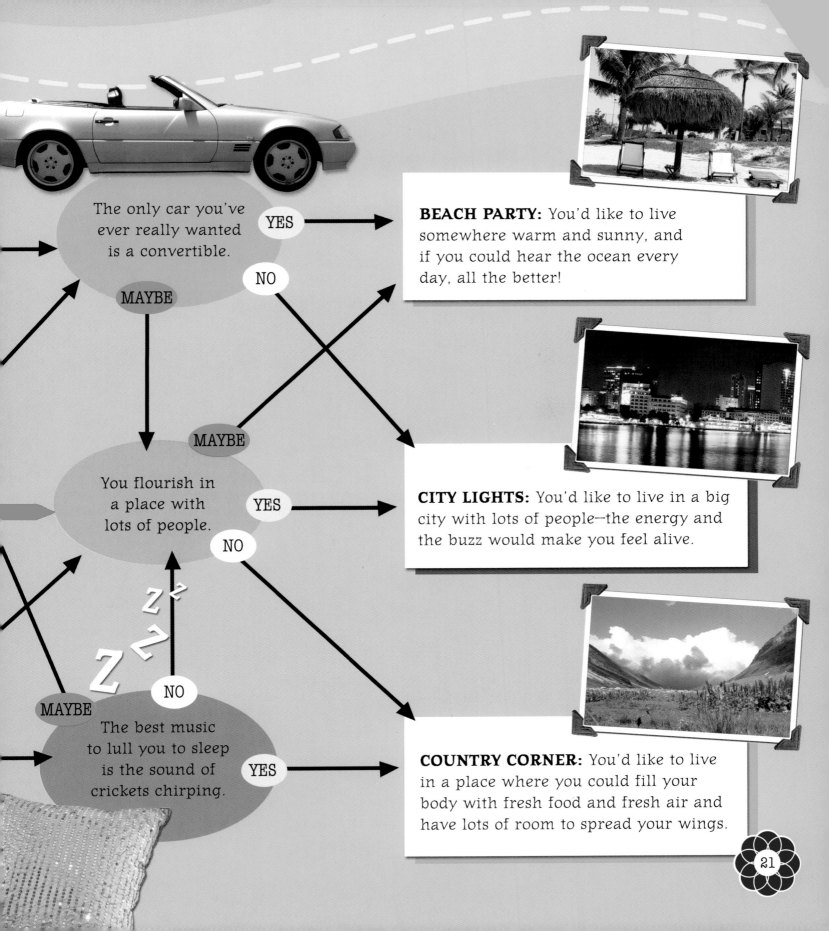

BEACH PARTY: You'd like to live somewhere warm and sunny, and if you could hear the ocean every day, all the better!

MAYBE

You flourish in a place with lots of people.

YES

NO

CITY LIGHTS: You'd like to live in a big city with lots of people—the energy and the buzz would make you feel alive.

MAYBE

NO

The best music to lull you to sleep is the sound of crickets chirping.

YES

COUNTRY CORNER: You'd like to live in a place where you could fill your body with fresh food and fresh air and have lots of room to spread your wings.

LET'S ALL HANG OUT

Miley, Lilly, and Oliver like to chil-lax at the beach, even if they do have to put up with Rico and pay for overpriced water at his surf shack. While the beach is great, it's not the only place to have fun. Answer the questions to see where you and your friends might want to go when you've got some downtime. Then check in with Miley and the gang and see where they'd like to go to kick back.

1 If you're hanging out and want to get food, you'd want to:

 check out the selection at the food court.

 check out the selection in the refrigerator.

 see if you can spot a pushcart vendor or snack shack.

2 To listen to some tunes together, you and your friends:

 check out the cool clothing stores where the music is blasting.

 play the latest downloads on your computer.

 head to the park with your iPods and share playlists.

3 You and your BFF want the sun-kissed look for an upcoming dance so you:

 go to the tanning boutique for a spray-on experience.

 do the self-tanning thing in your room.

 already have the look, since you're both outdoors all the time.

4 You and your friends love to:

 browse through the stores.

 make YouTube videos or play video games.

head to get a game going—beach volleyball, Frisbee, whatever.

5 If you need to take a break, you and your friends:

 sit in the massage chairs at the gadget store.

 watch TV.

sit under a shady tree and drink some water.

6

For your birthday it would be great if the 'rents got you:

 gift cards to your fave stores.

 a Foosball table.

 a mountain bike.

7

You'd like to be in a place where you could:

 see and be seen.

 have privacy.

 get some fresh air.

8

There's nothing you need to dress for, so you wear:

 your latest purchases.

 loungewear.

 whatever the weather calls for.

SCORING:

MOSTLY  'S: **The Mall.** You and your friends like to shop till you drop, then you'll refuel at the food court. And it's always fun to see who you'll meet on the weekends.

MOSTLY  'S: **Home Sweet Home.** You and your friends like to hang out at each other's houses. You can just be yourselves, with all the comforts of home.

MOSTLY  'S: **Park It.** You and your friends like to play wherever you can, so you're likely to want to hang out at a public park. It might be a beach, a skating rink, or a grassy playing field, as long as you can all join in the fun.

CALLING ALL CRUSHES

Would you rather go to the mall or check out the cute guys at the beach? That's an easy question for Miley and Lilly. (BTW the answer is: see the cute guys at the beach.) It's fun to crush on people. But who's the right crush for you? A sweet and sensitive guy or a guy that has you ROFL? Take the quiz, then check your score with Lilly or Miley or both to see if they agree.

1. You'd love it if your crush sent you a funny Valentine that made you laugh.
    YES — that would be perfect.
    MAYBE — whatever he picked would be fine—as long as it's from him.
    NO — you'd want something a little more romantic.

2. You'd love it if your crush sent texts with the joke of the day.
    YES — even the lame ones are worth a chuckle.
    MAYBE — if he thought they were really funny.
    NO — you'd rather have more personal messages.

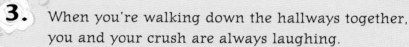

3. When you're walking down the hallways together, you and your crush are always laughing.
        YES — he cracks you up.
        MAYBE — if you're both in a good mood.
        NO — you're too busy gazing into each other's eyes.

4. You're walking by a kids' playground and your crush wants to go on the swings. Do you go with him?
        YES — you'll challenge him to see who can swing higher.
        MAYBE — if you feel like it, but it's okay if you don't.
        NO — only if there's a swing for two.

5. Your crush does a cannonball into the pool and soaks you on purpose. Do you laugh?
        YES — he's just being playful.
        MAYBE — as long as you were going in, anyway.
        NO — in fact, it would really bother you.

6. You'd love to stroll, hand in hand, through a carnival.
        YES — you'd both have fun playing the games and going on rides.
        MAYBE — as long as you'd be together.
        NO — you'd rather be someplace quiet where you can talk.

7. You're at a party that's kind of dull, so the host breaks out a karaoke machine.
Your crush wants to be the first one to give it a shot, even though he can't sing.
Do you encourage him?
        YES — it would be worth it to liven up the party.
        MAYBE — if he can turn it into a group sing-along.
        NO — you wouldn't want him to be embarrassed.

8. Your crush has to write a poem for English class. Would he turn in this silly rhyme?
I'm not a poet, don't tell me, I know it.
It's because I'm not very good, picking words like I should.
When your favorite color is purple, it's . . . kind of a problem.
        YES — he'd do it as a joke.
        MAYBE — you *think* the English teacher has a sense of humor.
        NO — he'd take the assignment seriously.

SCORING:
YES = 1 point
MAYBE = 2 points
NO = 3 points

8—13:
COMIC CUTIE.
Your crush is a guy that
keeps you laughing.
You're full of smiles
for him.

14—19:
FRIENDLY AND FUN.
Your crush is someone
who's fun, but he's also
aware of other people.
His down-to-earth style
is right up your alley.

20—24:
ROMANTIC ROMEO.
Your crush is sweet,
considerate, and more
on the serious side.
That's fine by you.

I Got Nerve (I think!)

IT TAKES a lot of nerve to get up onstage in front of a huge crowd and belt out your latest song. But Hannah Montana has what it takes! Would you get up onstage? What else do you have the nerve to try to do? Take the quiz and decide whether you would go for it or hold back. Then take the quiz again, but see what Hannah says instead.

1. Your school PTA is sponsoring an art contest. The winning entry will go on to a national contest. Do you submit your drawings even though you've never shown them to anybody before?

2. A cute new guy just transferred to your school—and he's in your class. Not only that, but he happens to sit right behind you in homeroom. Do you offer to show him around?

3. The community youth program is sponsoring a talent show. A friend wants to pull together a girl band. She wants everyone to dress up, dance, and lip-synch your favorite song. Do you join the band?

4. You never learned to ice-skate, but a friend is having a birthday party at a local ice arena. Your crush is going. Do you go to the party, too—even though your crush will see you clumsily clinging to the rink walls instead of gracefully gliding across the ice?

5. You hear one of the more popular girls in school gossiping about a good friend—and the rumor she's spreading is totally untrue. Do you speak up?

6. The auditions for the school play are next week. You've always wanted to try acting, but you know the drama teacher can be really tough. It might be a great learning experience, or a totally embarrassing one. Do you sign up?

7. You didn't make the travel soccer team last year. It's tryout time again. There are some openings on the team, but you know the rest of the players are really competitive. Do you try out?

8. Your neighbor is planning a fashion show as a charity fund-raiser. She asks you to be one of the models for the show, which will take place at the mall. Your neighbor mentions to your parents that she'll be choosing all the clothes herself. It's fine with your parents. But you have serious questions about your neighbor's sense of style. Do you agree to do it, anyway?

9. You have a great voice, and your principal wants you to sing the national anthem at the next school assembly. You've never sung in public before. Do you make your debut?

10. You love to make jewelry. All your friends love your pieces, and one offers to take some pictures and help you create a brochure to showcase your talent. Is it time to launch your own business?

HANNAH:
There are no right or wrong answers here—you need to do what you're comfortable doing.

you answered "yes" to
st *of these questions then you've*
nerves of steel! New experiences
ite *you. Even if everything*
sn't *work out exactly as*
nned, *that doesn't stop you*
n *trying again next time.*

If you answered "no" *to most of these questions then you like to stay on the safe side of things. That's fine, but don't be afraid to take a chance now and again. You'll probably surprise yourself when you see what you can really do!*

If you answered with a mix of "yes" and "no" or even "I don't know" *then you're ready to dive in when you think the reward is worth the risk. You know what's right for you, so follow your head and your heart!*

G.N.I. (GIRLS' NIGHT IN)

IT'S A girls' night out—in your house. After all, staying in can be as much fun as going out. You invite your best buds over to spend the night, but what should you plan to do? Follow the path to see which sleepover will keep everyone from falling asleep—then see if Lilly and Miley agree with the direction you're heading in.

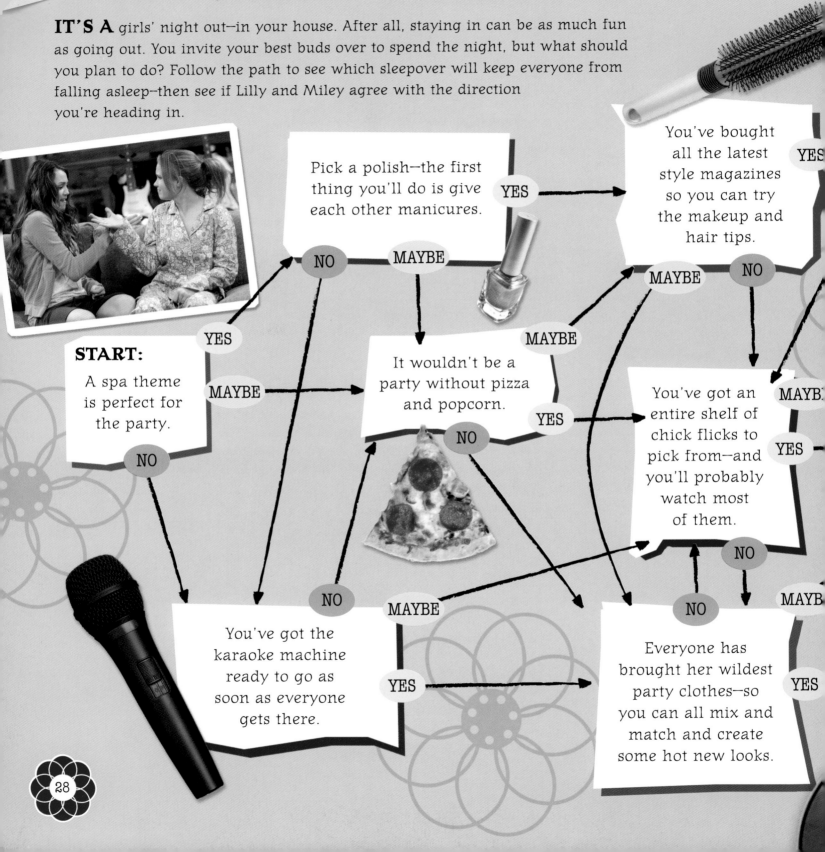

Pick a polish—the first thing you'll do is give each other manicures.

YES

You've bought all the latest style magazines so you can try the makeup and hair tips.

YES

NO

MAYBE

MAYBE

NO

YES

MAYBE

START:
A spa theme is perfect for the party.

MAYBE

It wouldn't be a party without pizza and popcorn.

MAYBE

NO

You've got an entire shelf of chick flicks to pick from—and you'll probably watch most of them.

MAYBE

YES

NO

YES

NO

You've got the karaoke machine ready to go as soon as everyone gets there.

NO

MAYBE

NO

MAYBE

Everyone has brought her wildest party clothes—so you can all mix and match and create some hot new looks.

YES

YES

28

MAYBE

It's a hairy-scary experience when everyone has her hair in rollers and face slathered in skin cream—so you take pictures!

YES

PAMPERING PARTY. Break out the nail polish, hairbrushes, and lipsticks! This party is all about making you and your friends look and feel good.

NO

NO

You'll all be drama queens as you act out the scenes.

YES

FOOD AND FLICKS. What can be more fun than watching a movie and eating popcorn in your pj's with all your BFFs around to enjoy the experience with you?

MAYBE

MAYBE

NO

Your friends show off their best moves as the music blares— and you make a great music video!

YES

DANCING DIVAS. It's time to get a little crazy— right in your own house. You and your fellow pop stars can dress up in your wildest clothes and dance the night away.

NOBODY'S PERFECT

Everyone has embarrassing moments. Miley might like to forget the time her pants blew up at the Make-a-Moose store, but Jackson probably won't let her. Even Hannah Montana has had some experiences that she'd like to forget, like the time she let herself be slimed instead of super-popular Amber at a singing contest. Nobody wants to be embarrassed, but it happens once in a while. When the spotlight is on you, do you melt? Or do you blush and take a bow, anyway? Answer yes or no to the questions below, then see what Miley and her crew would do in one of these wish-I-wasn't-here situations.

1. You and your mom are out shopping. She keeps pestering you to try out some of the clothes she's choosing. You finally do, just to make her happy. The first thing you try makes you look like you're a little kid. You walk out of the dressing room to show your mom—and spot your worst enemy with *her* mom. Even worse, her mom is chatting with your mom. Do you say anything?

YES — you smile sweetly and tell your mom, "I don't think this is me. Thanks, anyway."
NO — you duck back into the dressing room and wait for your mom to come to you.

2. At a weekend slumber party, you and your friends had fun adding streaks of color to your hair. You chose orange and pink. The product label said the color washes right out. But by Monday morning the color still hasn't faded. A quick check with your friends finds them all back to normal. Do you go to school?

YES — and dress in your best punk-rocker clothes.
NO — it's probably the one time your mom will let you spend the day in the beauty salon.

3. You're volunteering at a charity fair, and the coordinator asks if you will be the person that sits in the dunk tank. After a few dunks, you know your makeup will be all over your face and your hair will be ruined for the rest of the day. Do you do it, anyway?

YES — it's for a good cause and it'll be fun.
NO — but you offer to sell tickets for it.

You're with your friends when you bump into a girl you met at summer camp. She's really nice and you want to introduce her to your buds, but her name left your brain. Do you fess up?

YES — you'll just apologize for the brain lapse.

NO — you tell her the names of your friends and hope she tells them hers.

You are babysitting your little brother and he wants to play *Star Wars*. The two of you are having a light-saber battle in the front yard when your crush walks by and starts watching! Do you ask him to join in?

YES — the Force is with you.

NO — you tell your brother you need a break and explain to your crush that you're babysitting.

You're daydreaming in math class when a friend pokes you. The teacher has just asked you to solve a problem. Do you admit you were spacing by asking her to repeat the question?

YES — better to get the answer right than to take a wild guess.

NO — better to guess than be embarrassed.

If most of your answers were
YES,
your self-confidence helps you handle embarrassing situations with a laugh and a smile. You've got nerve!

If you were split between
YES and **NO,**
then you're sure of yourself sometimes, but slightly shy other times. Keep a smile on your face and you'll be okay!

If most of your answers were
NO,
then you're usually pretty aware of the reactions of other people. Just remember that nobody's perfect. Try to laugh at your own mistakes and remember that embarrassing things happen to everyone!

SONGWRITER CENTRAL

ROBBY RAY is more than a great dad who likes to tell stories about Uncle Earl. He's also a songwriter, using his special guitar to write the songs that his daughter sings as Hannah Montana. But what if Robby Ray wrote a song for you? What kind of song would you want him to compose? Answer the questions and go where the music takes you to find out. Then walk along the path with Miley to see if she comes up with the same answers.

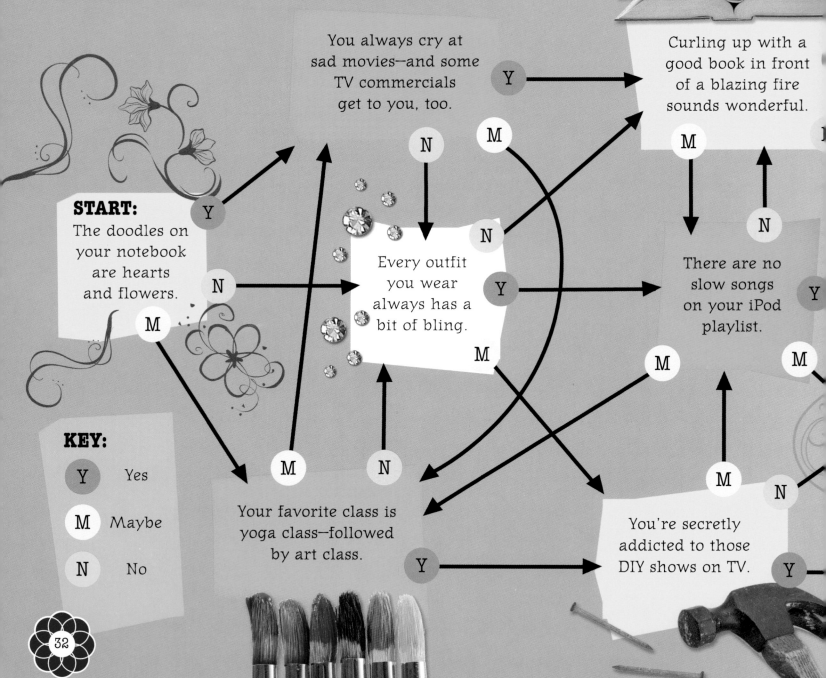

You always cry at sad movies—and some TV commercials get to you, too.

Curling up with a good book in front of a blazing fire sounds wonderful.

START:
The doodles on your notebook are hearts and flowers.

Every outfit you wear always has a bit of bling.

There are no slow songs on your iPod playlist.

KEY:

Y — Yes

M — Maybe

N — No

Your favorite class is yoga class—followed by art class.

You're secretly addicted to those DIY shows on TV.

Your favorite lip gloss color is pink. **Y** → **A SOFT LOVE SONG.** You are a romantic at heart, so a beautiful ballad would make you melt.

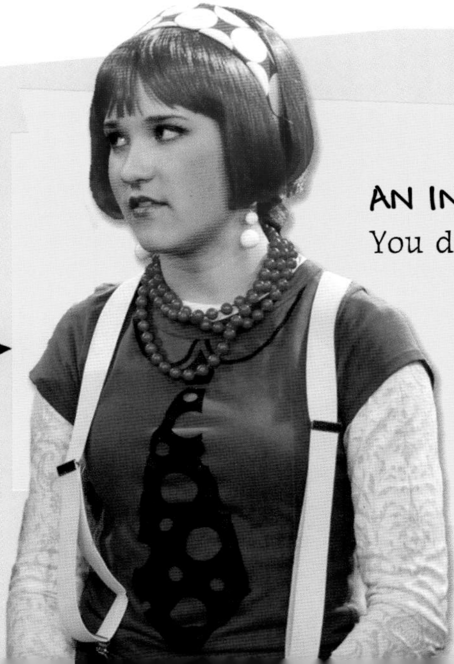

M

N

You love to get your nails painted with cool designs. **Y** → **AN UPBEAT POP SONG.** You're ready for fun, so you'd want a tune that would make you move.

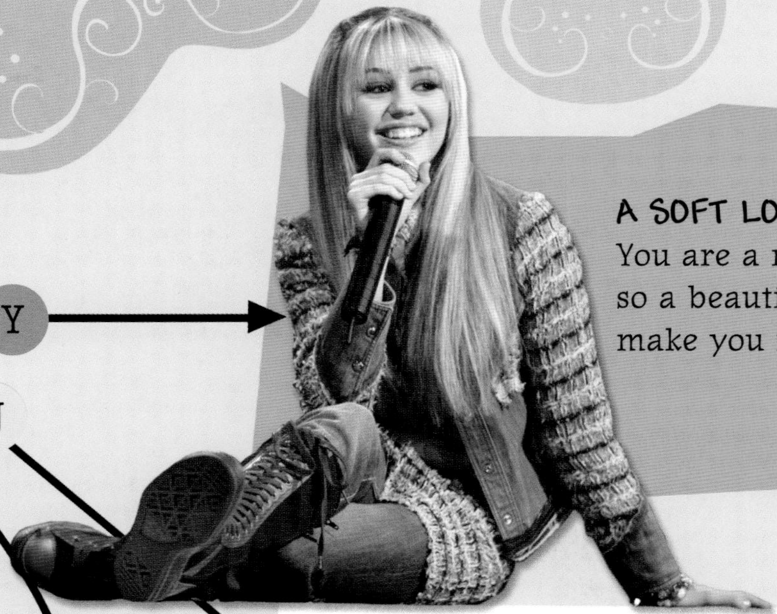

M

N

N

You need to make your own jewelry—the stores never seem to have anything that fits your style. **Y** → **AN INDIE ROCK SONG.** You don't follow the crowd—so a song that's not in the mainstream is right up your alley.

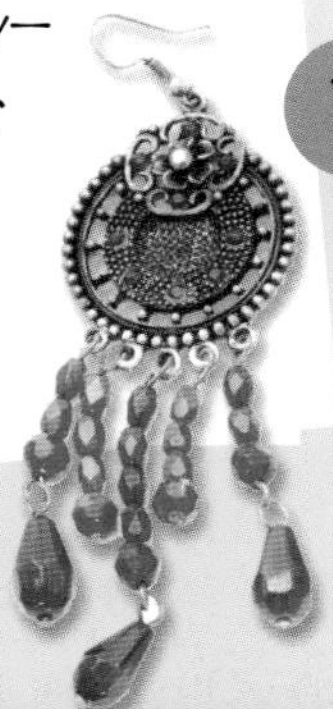

M

N THE (AMAZING) ROAD AGAIN

All aboard! Hannah Montana is hitting the road and going on a concert tour! One of the cool benefits of being a pop star is getting to travel around and see new places. But if you were kicking off your concert tour, where would you start? Since your fans everywhere are great, you can decide based on what else you can see while you're there! Then see if Hannah is okay with double billing as you start your tour together.

1. You would love to have tea:
   A. with the queen.
   B. in the Russian Tea Room.
   C. in a special ceremony.

2. It would be amazing to get tickets to see:
   A. a football game at Wembley Stadium.
   B. a basketball game at Madison Square Garden.
   C. a baseball game at the Tokyo Dome.

3. You're in a seafood mood, so for lunch you'd like to try:
   A. fish and chips.
   B. lox and bagels.
   C. sushi.

4. You'd be most excited by the neon lights of:
   A. Piccadilly Circus.
   B. Times Square.
   C. Shibuya.

5. For fresh air and exercise, you'd like to walk around:
   A. Kensington Gardens.
   B. Central Park.
   C. Imperial Palace Gardens.

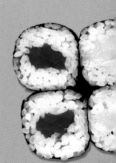

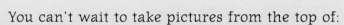

HANNAH SAYS: It really doesn't matter where you start—I had never heard of half of these places until I looked them up on the Internet. And I learned that each city is special in its own way—so I plan to visit them all!

6. You can't wait to take pictures from the top of:
- **A.** the London Eye.
- **B.** the Empire State Building.
- **C.** Tokyo Tower.

7. If you were feeling reflective you'd visit:
- **A.** Westminster Abbey.
- **B.** Saint Patrick's Cathedral.
- **C.** Asakusa Kannon Temple.

8. You'd really like to spend some time window shopping:
- **A.** as you walk down Oxford Street.
- **B.** as you stroll down Fifth Avenue.
- **C.** as you amble through the Ginza Shopping District.

MOSTLY A's:
Cheerio! London, England, is the place where you can start your tour!

MOSTLY C's:
Visit the land of the rising sun and start your concert tour in Toyko, Japan. *Sayonara!*

MOSTLY B's:
Begin your tour in the Big Apple, New York City! And give your regards to Broadway.

P-A-R-T-Y

Hannah Montana gets invited to some great parties, so she has met lots of celebrities! But a party doesn't have to be star-studded to be a lot of fun. And to make sure you get an invite, why not think about hosting a party of your own? But before you can start party planning, you need to decide what kind of party you would like to throw.

No one knows more about parties than Oliver. (At least, he thinks he does.) So check to see if Oliver agrees with your choices—if not, see what kind of par-tay the O-man picks for you.

1. To get everyone the party 411, you would:
   a. mail engraved invitations.
   b. send a text.
   c. make flyers with all the details and hand them out. The more the merrier.

2. To answer the big pre-party question, "What should I wear?" you'd tell people:
   a. wear something elegant.
   b. wear something funky.
   c. wear something comfortable.

3. When a guest arrives, he or she might want to try:
   a. one of the fancy appetizers.
   b. the spicy salsa and chips.
   c. a hamburger or salad.

4. The perfect setting for your dream party would be:
   a. a lavish yacht.
   b. a big dance floor with a disco ball.
   c. a big beach house with an outdoor patio.

5. Every party needs music, so you'd hire:
   a. a string quartet or a pianist.
   b. an MC and a DJ.
   c. a band that rocks.

6. Your guests would arrive:
   a. in limousines.
   b. in cars or taxis.
   c. whatever, as long as they get there.

7. Mood lighting would be provided by:
   a. candles and tiny white lights.
   b. colorful strobes that flash to the beat.
   c. a bonfire and the starry sky.

MOSTLY A'S: Your fantasy party would be an elegant event, complete with ice sculptures, designer dresses, and an A-list guest list.

MOSTLY B'S: Your dream would be to host a happening dance party that got all of your guests moving their feet to the beat.

MOSTLY C'S: You'd hope to have a huge blowout with as many people as possible! It would be casual but lots of fun!

WORKIN' FOR A LIVIN'

Working for Rico is no day at the beach—just ask Jackson. So maybe it's time for him to look for a new job. But what about you? If you wanted to make some extra cash over the summer, what kind of job would be right for you? Check with Jackson's business partner in the cheeze-jerky business, Oliver, to see if you're on the road to riches, or will at least make enough money to go to the movies.

1. Your friends always admire how clean and neat your locker looks.

   YES — you hate clutter.
   MAYBE — it's not always neat, but it's always decorated.
   NO — you don't mind a little mess.

2. The folders you use in school are color-coded for each subject.

   YES — it makes it easy to find the one you need.
   MAYBE — you've doodled a lot on them so it's hard to tell.
   NO — but you manage, anyway.

3. You have no problem chatting with teachers and coaches.

   YES — you actually like talking to adults.
   MAYBE — you'd rather talk to kids your own age.
   NO — but you're great with little kids.

4. You don't mind being in one place all day.

   YES — as long as your mind is busy, you're happy.
   MAYBE — you'd need to move around a little bit.
   NO — you'd need to move around a lot.

5. You plan to make your holiday wish list a PowerPoint presentation.

   YES — everyone will appreciate how easy it is to understand.
   MAYBE — if it turns into a fashion slide show.
   NO — you like to do these things by hand.

6. You don't mind wearing dress clothes every day.

   YES — dressing up is fun.

   MAYBE — as long as the clothing can be cutting edge, too.

   NO — you'd rather be in a T-shirt and shorts in the summer.

7. Your room has lots of organized shelves.

   YES — it's great to have your stuff at your fingertips.

   MAYBE — the baskets are overflowing with accessories.

   NO — there are more arts and crafts scattered everywhere than anything else.

8. When your friends send you pictures, you download and sort the pics into e-scrapbooks.

   YES — you print out the pages and impress everyone.

   MAYBE — you use the pages to decorate your closet door.

   NO — you just print out the pics and make your own frames.

SCORING:

1 point for every YES, 2 points for every MAYBE, and 3 points for every NO.

If your score was between 8 and 12, you're an OFFICE ORGANIZER! The boss would love your ease with computers, your organizational skills, and your professional manner.

If your score was between 13 and 18, you're a BOUTIQUE BABE! Shoppers would flock to you for tips on the latest styles and the latest sales.

If your score was between 19 and 24, you'd make a GREAT CAMP COUNSELOR! Working with younger kids doing arts and crafts, outdoor activities, and generally having fun would make work a pleasure.

IF WE WERE A MOVIE...HERE'S THE KIND IT WOULD BE

With Jake's filming schedule and Miley's secret life as Hannah, it was hard for the two of them to find time to spend together. So the first thing you and your crush need to do is pencil each other into your busy schedules. But then what? If someone were to make a movie starring the two of you, what kind would it be? Answer each question and follow the path to find out. Then check in with Miley to see if she agrees.

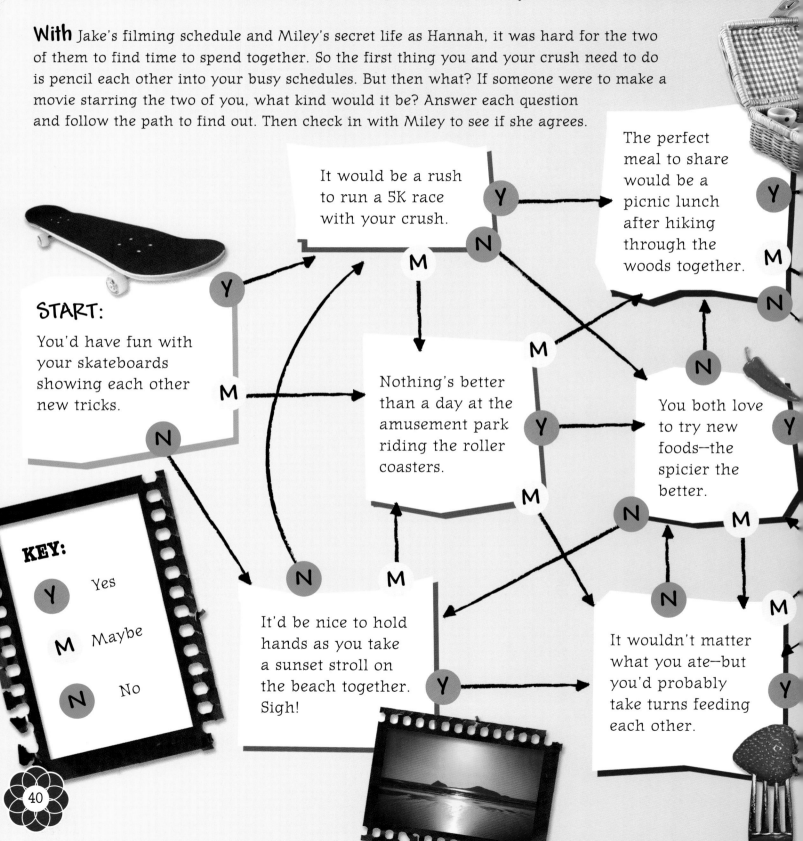

It would be a rush to run a 5K race with your crush.

The perfect meal to share would be a picnic lunch after hiking through the woods together.

START:

You'd have fun with your skateboards showing each other new tricks.

Nothing's better than a day at the amusement park riding the roller coasters.

You both love to try new foods—the spicier the better.

KEY:

Y   Yes

M   Maybe

N   No

It'd be nice to hold hands as you take a sunset stroll on the beach together. Sigh!

It wouldn't matter what you ate—but you'd probably take turns feeding each other.

40

On a summer's day at the public pool, you'd challenge your crush to a swimming race.

Y →

M

N

A SPORTS FLICK.
You and your crush love to be active and compete against each other. But you also work together to take your sporting skills to the next level.

M

On a summer's day at the public pool, you and your crush would take turns jumping off the springboard.

Y →

M

N

AN ADVENTURE FILM.
You and your crush love to get thrills from trying new things together—it's all fun.

M

On a summer's day at the public pool, you and your crush would just lounge in the sun together holding hands.

Y →

A DATE MOVIE.
You and your crush like to do romantic things—walks on the beach, sending each other cards and notes, and just being together.

I've Got a Secret

(Secret Celebrity / Part-time Pop Star)

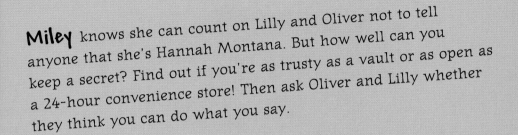

Miley knows she can count on Lilly and Oliver not to tell anyone that she's Hannah Montana. But how well can you keep a secret? Find out if you're as trusty as a vault or as open as a 24-hour convenience store! Then ask Oliver and Lilly whether they think you can do what you say.

1. Your friend got an ugly sweater for her birthday from an aunt who lives far away. You know this friend also happens to be short on cash, but you're surprised to see her give the sweater to someone else as a gift. Do you spill to the new owner of the ugly sweater?

2. You and your BFF discover a new second-hand shop that is selling some amazing clothes for practically nothing! The next day at school, other kids compliment you on your new clothes. You're eager to advertise the store, but your friend wants to keep the new shop a secret for as long as possible. Do you keep your lips sealed?

3. You know two of your friends are crushing on the same guy. He asks one of them to go out, and she accepts. But she wants to be the one to break the news to your other friend after school. Do you text the other friend before then?

4. Your friend split her jeans! She's draped a hoodie around her waist, so she's covered. But you keep cracking up! (It is funny—even your friend admits it.) Do you let a few people in on the "cover-up"?

5. A BFF is bummed because she thinks everyone has forgotten her birthday. There's a big surprise party planned for that night. Do you hint around that maybe everyone didn't forget?

6. You and your friends go to a pool party. A friend says she doesn't want to go into the water because it's too cold, but you know it's because she can't swim. Do you tell everyone and hand her a pair of Floaties?

7. You saw an awesome movie over the weekend—it was full of suspense and the ending had a great twist. You want to talk about it at school, but one of your friends hasn't seen the film yet. Do you talk about it, anyway?

8. You know where your parents have hidden your brother's birthday present. His birthday is tomorrow, but he's dying to know if they bought him an Xbox 360. He swears he'll act surprised when he opens the present, no matter what. Do you reveal the location of the loot?

Score 1 point for every **YES** answer, then tally your points and see how you rate as a keeper of secrets.

0-2: You are a locked vault—so any secret is pretty safe with you!

3-5: You have some secret slips. Sometimes you can manage to keep a secret in . . . and sometimes you can't.

6-8: You're an open book. When you've got news, it's just too hard to keep it in.

GET THE PARTY PUMPIN'

Hannah likes all kinds of music—not just her own! And she loves to dance. What kind of music gets your body pumpin'? And when you move to the music, what kinds of dancing do you enjoy most? Then see what Hannah thinks about your dancing—maybe you're ready to be one of her backup dancers!

1. To you "put on your dancing shoes" means:

    grabbing ballet slippers or taps.

    lacing up your favorite sneakers.

    putting on a pair of pretty heels.

2. You like it when the crowd:

    applauds your performance.

    makes room for you and your partner to glide across the floor.

    is dancing along with you.

3. You'd like to wear a dance costume made from:

    satin and tulle.

    silk and sequins.

    the clothes in your closet.

4. If you get thirsty after dancing you'll want to sip:

    spring water with a slice of lemon.

    fruit punch with two straws.

    an energy drink.

5. You think it would be fun to:

 go on a national tour with a dance company.

 take part in a ballroom dance competition on TV.

 make a music video with your fave R & B artist.

6. As you move to the music you feel:

 beautiful.

 fiery.

 energized.

7. The musical instruments you listen for are:

 violins and flutes.

 the brass section.

 drums and the bass.

8. When others watch you dance, they'll be blown away by your:

 gracefulness.

 fancy footwork.

 creativity.

There are LOTS of different styles of dancing. There are also different ethnic dances, like belly dancing, hula dancing, or Irish step dancing. So take a chance and DANCE however, wherever, and whenever you can!

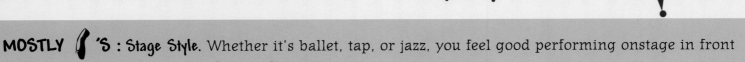

MOSTLY 's : Stage Style. Whether it's ballet, tap, or jazz, you feel good performing onstage in front of an audience.

MOSTLY 's : It Takes Two. From ballroom and swing dancing to some south-of-the-border sizzle with salsa dancing, your favorite moves are with a partner.

MOSTLY 's : Dance Club Dazzle. From hip-hop moves to popping and locking, you've got the rhythm of the street moving through your feet.

Who Said?

THE QUESTIONS NEVER END ... but this book has to. So here are a few last questions for Miley and her friends. What do they see in your future? Ask the "What'cha Think?" device to find out. But don't forget the message of Hannah's music: You always have a choice, and you lead your own parade. So no matter what anyone says, do it your way! BBFN!

Will I win any awards?
Will I ever be on TV?
Will I ever get concert tickets?
Do I rock—at least sometimes?

Is my BFF hiding something?
Should I try a new sport?
Will I get faster at texting?
Should I cut my hair?

Should I change my ring tone?
Will my game improve?
Should I join a new club?
Should I work on my dance moves?

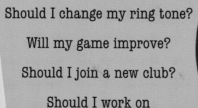

Does my crush have a crush on me?
Should I plan a girls' night out?
Will I remember to turn in my homework?
Do I need a manicure?